PIG the ELF

Aaron Blabey

Scholastic Canada Ltd.
Toronto New York London Auckland Sydney
Mexico City New Delhi Hong Kong Buenos Aires

Oh, Christmas Eve!
That most merry of nights!
The carols! The baubles!
The small twinkly lights!

Santa was coming!
'Twas bigger than big,
but no one was feeling
more festive than . . .

PIG!

How he loved Christmas!
He'd chortle with glee—
"The presents! The presents!
For ME! ME! ME! ME!"

He'd written his list,
and he'd asked for a lot.
But Santa takes orders,
so why on earth not?

I WANT:
A MOTORBIKE
A ROCKET
A DRUMKIT
A PONY
A SKATEBOARD
A CANDY FLOSS
MAKER
A TRA

Dear Santa,
May I please have
something nice
for Christmas?
from Trevor
PS-I love yo

He just couldn't wait.
He was itching for loot.
He could barely sit still
in his little red suit.

"The presents! The presents!"
he muttered again.
"*When* will he get here?
Oh, WHEN?
TELL ME WHEN?!"

"He'll come when we sleep," said his lovely friend Trevor.

But Pig shouted, "SLEEP? I'll have none whatsoever!"

"Sleep is for fools!
Oh yes, sleep is for losers!
I won't go to bed
with the rest of you snoozers!

"I'm sitting up late!
I'll be here when he comes!
I swear by these stockings
and gingerbread crumbs!"

So Trevor went dutifully
off to his bed.

But naughty old Pig
stayed up just like he said.

The waiting was endless,
but Pig held his ground.
Then at three thirty-three,
well, he heard a strange sound . . .

And who should appear
down the chimney with swag,
but a portly old gent
with a lumpy red bag.

He piled up some presents
marked "Trevor" and "Pig,"
then he picked up his milk
and he took a quick swig.

But then, as he turned
to go back on his way,

Trevor

Pig

a short cranky dog appeared,
shouting out,

"HEY!"

"I asked for MORE!
bellowed Pig in dismay.
But Santa turned tail
and was scuttling away.

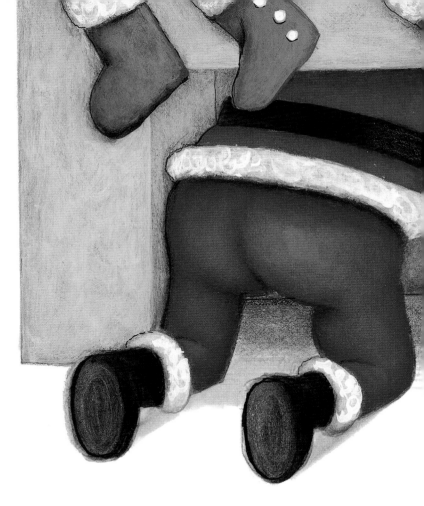

"HEY!" shouted Pig,
"I'm not done with you, chum!"

Then he nipped poor old Santa's
big rosy red bum!

Up through the chimney . . .

Out to the sleigh . . .

Pig held on tight.
"You're not getting away!
I asked for a mountain
of presents and loot!
So where is the rest,

YOU OLD YULETIDE GALOOT?!"

But the sleigh took off fast.

Gee, those reindeer were speedy!

And away fell their guest—

Yes, the one who was greedy.

But as Trevor lay dreaming
of holiday cheer,
a real Christmas miracle
happened right here . . .

Yes, Pig must be blessed.
He survived that big drop,
and was saved by a tree . . .

. . . with an angel on top.